OTTO the CAT

ISBN 0-590-92882-1

Text copyright © 1995 by Gail Herman.
Illustrations copyright © 1995 Norman Gorbaty.
All rights reserved. Published by Scholastic Inc., 555 Broadway, New York, NY 10012, by arrangement with Grosset & Dunlap, Inc., a member of The Putnam & Grosset Group.

12 11 10 9 8 7 6 5 4 3 2 1   6 7 8 9/9 0 1/0

Printed in the U.S.A.   24

First Scholastic printing, September 1996

A PICTURE READER

OTTO the CAT

By Gail Herman
Illustrated by Norman Gorbaty

Scholastic Inc.

New York   Toronto   London   Auckland   Sydney

Otto is a  .

He lives in a  .

"My  ," says Otto.

He has a .

"My ," says Otto.

Otto even has a .

Today Otto wants to go

to the pet store.

What does Otto want?

He wants a new .

He wants

a new toy .

Otto gets everything

he wants.

Does he want a  ?

No!

Too late!

The  wants Otto.

He wags his  .

"Out of my  !"

says Otto.

The  stays put.

"Out of my !"

says Otto.

The stays put.

"Out of my  !"

Otto tells the  .

"Do not play with

my toy  .

Do not eat from

my blue  ."

What can Otto do?

Everywhere he goes,

the  goes too.

All at once,

Otto knows what to do.

He runs out of the

to the .

The  runs too!

I will run

around and around.

I will make the

 dizzy.

Then I will run back.

And he will not find

<u>my</u> .

Otto runs around.

At last, he stops.

Otto is dizzy.

But is the  dizzy?

No!

The  is not

dizzy at all.

He picks Otto up.

He takes him to

the .

"My ," says Otto.

"My 🚗.

My blue 🥣.

My toy 🐭.

My 🛏."

Otto looks at the  .

"<u>My</u> ," says Otto.

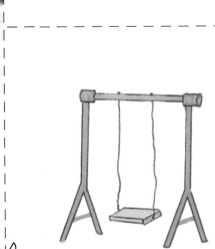
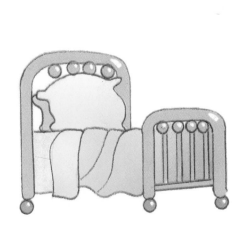

mouse	cat
house	dog
bed	swing

tail	car
barn	bowl
clown	book

The Little Engine That Could™

duck	bus
star	trees
table	train

apple	bike
sun	cake
truck	ball